Also by Paul Kiritsis

*Origin: Poems from the crack of dawn*

*Hermetica: Myths, Legends, Poems*

# Fifty Confessions

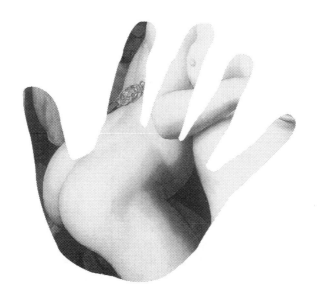

## Paul Kiritsis

iUniverse, Inc.
New York  Bloomington

*Fifty Confessions*

Copyright © 2009 by Paul Kiritsis

*iUniverse books may be ordered through booksellers or by contacting:*

*iUniverse
1663 Liberty Drive
Bloomington, IN 47403
www.iuniverse.com
1-800-Authors (1-800-288-4677)*

Because of the dynamic nature of the Internet, any Web addresses or links contained in
this book may have changed since publication and may no longer be valid. The views
expressed in this work are solely those of the author and do not necessarily reflect the
views of the publisher, and the publisher hereby disclaims any responsibility for them.

*ISBN: 978-1-4401-2449-5 (pbk)
ISBN: 978-1-4401-2448-8 (cloth)
ISBN: 978-1-4401-2450-1 (ebk)*

*Printed in the United States of America*

*iUniverse rev. date: 3/11/2009*

*For my brother*
*Dimitrios*

*My Lord, give me reason to carry on*

*When I find myself dishonored,*

*Stripped of all dignity,*

*Standing at the last frontier*

*Before a swift surrender*

*To an abyss of no return*

*To bottomless fears*

*That life will refuse me my right*

*To dream and hope*

*As a being of the light,*

*To aspire and just be.*

*My Lord, what is there left to do?*

*At most, I beseech your flame*

*Continue to burn within,*

*For I fear tomorrow*

*I shall awake*

*Without You,*

*And all grace will be lost.*

# Contents

# Acknowledgments

What began as a personal crisis that threatened my worldview, my ideals, my love, my aspirations, my very Self (and nearly overturned it completely), spilled itself, with an inky heart, onto leafy sheets and culminated as a compendium of fifty confessions.

These private confessions (at times solemn and contemplative, at others seething with resentment, and at others yet again touched with the faint tinge of hope), would never have seen the light of day or poured their souls onto print had it not been for an ancient enemy— intangible, subtle, yet very real—taking firm root in the depths of my being.

In order to ascend, we must first descend. This is divine logic and common sense, yet we scarcely understand it.

Far from a solitary endeavor, I was not alone in steering my own Titanic away from precipitous icebergs. I revel in pride and honor at this chance to thank my crew personally, one by one.

My first expression of gratitude belongs with my cousin, Harry Toulacis, for his continued support and belief in me. Harry, you were a fundamental asset to this work, providing endless suggestions on the book's content and structure. You were also a spring that gushed forth with optimism, hope, and fraternal love when I was in desperate need and thirsty for such. My gratitude to you knows no end.

Janet Christie, my close friend and work colleague at NYCH, for her unyielding passion, enthusiasm, and inspiration. Of the infinite things that unite us, I cherish your love the most. Both of us still have many more life lessons to learn from Tibetan monk Lobsang Rampa—we'll get there in the end, even if the ship ends up marooned on an outcrop of rocks. The prayer at the beginning of the book is dedicated to you.

Janice McGlinchey, my dear friend, who has also endured a nightmarish ordeal and has had to face some of her very own demons in the last few years. Thank you for your keen ear, the stimulating conversations over endless cups of brewed coffee, and the clinical work we did together that was imperative to my psychic healing. Salvation is just around the corner—I'm sure of it.

Barbara Hoare, my beloved friend and a GP worthy of being cast a saint, thank you for your words of advice and tireless striving for my care and well-being. You are always in my heart.

This is the third time I'm able to thank my editor, Paul Bugeja, for his work on my manuscript—but most importantly, for his support throughout a few months of very dark days when sunlight was all but present.

My mother and father, Chryssoula and Christos, for their inexorable love and support: I thank you always.

Finally, my last and most heartfelt acknowledgment goes to the Lord through which we all live, strive for, suffer, love, experience the world, find meaning in, and have our being. Please don't desert the tabernacle on the mast of my ship.

# Author's Note

Sometime near the end of May 2008, I had a distressing nightmare so potent that I was unable to shake off a very disquieting feeling it created in me for days after.

In the nightmare, I remember just wearing shorts and a sleeveless, red T-shirt, walking along a promenade in a city unrecognizable to me. Suddenly, I was stopped by a passerby who pointed out that my body was covered in deep sores and wounds, some of which looked like the perfectly elliptical ones in Swiss cheese. Indeed, when I peered down, my torso was riddled with fleshy wounds penetrating through to the bones. I was too scared to yank my shirt up and examine the rest of my torso because I instinctively knew what I would see. "How unusual," the stranger said. "You should really be dead by now, shouldn't you." He spoke this more as a statement than a question.

I awoke with a muffled scream, my skin crawling. This dream, more than any other, had seemed so potent, so real, as if it had actually happened. It reminded me of various nightmares filled with rotting body parts that I'd dreamt earlier in the year.

I'm not superstitious as such, although I am a believer in the raw power of the unconscious to discern and bring to conscious awareness various unaddressed issues and underlying fears, and to a degree, to predict the future. This dream felt like a premonition—a warning that something was going to go horribly wrong very soon. Would something be threatened? Was I going to fall gravely ill? Would I awake one day, powerless, hanging onto a thread of sanity, to find my life had been overturned? Whatever the dream meant, it wouldn't leave me; it just hovered around the back of my head like some nagging swarm of bees in the days that followed.

On the fourth of June, I crashed. I began having severe cognitive difficulties and experienced photophobia. The problems ranged from memory loss, confusion, and the inability to hold more than a few minutes of concentration, to brain fuzziness, loss of organizational skills, and difficulty in word retrieval. I'd always had sensitive eyes, but this sudden, acute worsening of my vision, which made voluminous objects impossible to look at, was constant and unrelenting. I also noted that the symptoms worsened during rigorous physical activity. The disintegration in physical heath was marked by a loss of interest in my day-to-day affairs. I no longer wanted to go to work, ceased going to the gym, and terminated my greatest love—writing. Nothing interested or engaged me.

In the weeks that followed, I became bedridden. The four general practitioners, two physicians, and all the emergency doctors at a local hospital that tended me could no more shed light on my condition than I could on how the indigenous peoples of Easter Island built the giant Moai statues. Extensive medical examinations found nothing. According to them, I was a perfectly healthy and fit twenty-nine-year-old male, suffering from a mild case of hypochondria. One told me that looking for a "magic cure" was fruitless; another that "medicine didn't have the answer to everything." Apart from their inability to help, their pessimism did little to lift my spirits.

I decided to take matters into my own hands, to distract myself from the hullabaloo of it all by spending some time in the countryside, away from the merciless and accelerating grind of the city, where I could clear my head and ruminate. It seemed to be of some help. Getting that much-needed fresh air into my lungs was also nice.

I began seeking aid elsewhere. Janice, an expert in clinical hypnotherapy, was of considerate help here, putting me under and then employing some relaxation and healing techniques on my aching psyche. We also did a substantial amount of work in the area of past-life regression, which was intensely stimulating. I also took the time to visit a close confidante of mine who happened to be a GP herself and had recently moved to the countryside—the wonderful Barbara Hoare. Together, we sat down for hours on end in intensive thought and speculation, and eventually she was able to narrow it down to a few possibilities. I figured I needed to do whatever was humanely possible to salvage what was left of my sanity, otherwise I would spiral down into an abyss from which there might be no return.

In order for one to fully understand the dire seriousness of my claims, it is important that I give you the complete story, which happens to be roughly sixteen years in length.

It began sometime during the summer of January 1992. I recall I had just returned from a family vacation to Adelaide and Mildura, reveling in the aftermath of much excitement of the trip up north, which had spawned my first experiences of handling live animals at a farm. All nervousness aside, I was even looking forward to my first year of high school. But shortly after we returned, something very bizarre happened.

It came on gradually, perhaps over the course of a week. I woke up one morning feeling somehow not myself. Suddenly, things *didn't feel right within me* anymore. There was a *wrongness* where prior there had been none. Something had changed. I couldn't put my finger on it; I didn't know what it was—how could I? I was but a child of twelve years old. The only thing I knew was that I wasn't as I had been. The thought gnawed away at my heart, physically aching like a headache. It still does. It's something that's incredibly difficult to describe without the conventional psychiatric connotations that go with this mode of expression. But make no mistake, there was nothing imagined or emotional about what was happening to me. It was as real and tangible as the air we breathe and the water we drink.

A few weeks later, I was watching the Australian Open with my grandmother. At its conclusion, I started flicking through the channels in the hope that something of interest would be on for late-night viewing. My attention was immediately seized by a horde of individuals huddled together, holding candles. Some of them were being interviewed by a reporter. When I increased the volume, I realized it was a program on people living with HIV, a virus which at that point in time was deemed an undisputed death sentence. It was engaging, so I decided to watch the rest of it.

You might imagine my horror when a young man of about twenty-five began describing what he called a *wrongness* inside him upon having been diagnosed HIV positive. At that point, I felt the onset of gooseflesh, a lurching stomach, and the blood drain completely from my face. I must have looked like a starved vampire who hasn't feasted in months. I vividly remember dashing into the bathroom and staring at my reflection in the mirror. Was this what was wrong with me?

Was I HIV positive?

I spent the next few hours crying and wondering what I'd done to deserve a fate like this. Why had God condemned me to an early death at such a young age? It was unfair, unjust. I lay awake that night, and many others, praying to the Virgin Mary, hoping that none of it was true. At one time, I even tried to convince myself that I'd made it all up and that it was nothing more than an illusion—that I'd never seen the show on TV about AIDS.

In hindsight, I'd rate it as the most traumatic moment of my life.

From that moment on, I made every effort to attend Sunday church and put forth my myriad questions to the saints and little baby Jesus. You might ask if I got my answers. To be honest, I'm not really sure. What I can say for certain is that an influx of hope and faith suddenly came from somewhere. Try as I might to shake the idea that I was dying, it became firmly rooted in my mind, and I spent endless nights cursing my fate, swearing and taking out my frustrations on a punching bag that hung from the roof of my old garage. I never dared to confess any of my secrets to our local priest; I felt that he wouldn't understand. What was happening to me was beyond comprehension.

In the years that followed, symptoms of constant tiredness and exhaustion manifested. I'm quite certain now that these were psychosomatic. I decided to drown all that had happened in my early teens into a well somewhere deep in the recesses of my unconscious. I then put up a brick wall between myself and HIV—I would have nothing to do with it. I cringed at any mention of the word *AIDS*.

My thinking became increasingly warped with the passage of time. Seen through the telescope of my own distorted perceptions on my own planet earth, diseases couldn't hurt me if I didn't know about them or if my diagnosis remained unconfirmed. The moment a general practitioner confirmed my dormant suspicions with the words "you're positive," the illusory protective spell would be broken, and I would die from grief—I was sure of it. Hearsay of terminally ill people living quite normal and healthy lives in ignorant bliss of their ailments upheld my, by then, well-established worldview.

For a while, life seemed to return to normal, and I even found myself attending regular confession at the local Greek Orthodox Church. But years of having kept my darkest fears sealed with a plug of silence deep down in my unconscious finally caught up with me. Just before I turned twenty-one, my physical symptoms worsened to the point where I was left with no choice but to request a full blood examination. You might imagine the pleasant shock when my HIV test came back negative. I remember being somewhat confused. Had I stupidly been living with an irrational fear for all those years without good reason? Was the wrongness that I felt and that which the guy on the AIDS documentary had described just a blind coincidence? If it wasn't HIV, then what did I have? What else could it have been?

I understood perfectly well that HIV wasn't at all easy to contract because there had to be an indefinite mingling of blood or semen from an infected person. I had, however, heard of unusual cases from people who tested positive yet who swore they'd never shared needles or had unprotected sex or undergone blood transfusions. In time, I found that my worries hadn't abated in the aftermath of these pleasant revelations. Why? For one, the physiological feeling of *wrongness* was still there. In addition, short bursts of photophobia and a generally increased sensitivity to light also manifested, particularly at night.

If HIV wasn't the culprit, what was? An unknown enemy is a much greater adversity than a known one; an explicit diagnosis better than an indefinite one. Why? Because to know something by name means you have knowledge of it, and knowledge of something allows you some power over it, however little that might be. Providing they exist, relevant weapons can also be assembled for biological warfare. Diagnosis "X," on the other hand, is much more unsettling because the enigma unfolds as a race against time to identify the microscopic assailant and address it.

The years rolled by without relief. I fell into depression during the time after my graduation because I failed to attain the TER score required to study Arts at Melbourne University. I settled instead for Behavioral Science at Latrobe University, betraying my gut instinct to study Arts at a different university. However, there was more to the depression than just marks; I could feel something else brewing within. My health was worsening. The *wrongness* was beginning to change somehow. It was getting worse. I felt that whatever was inside me was multiplying, proliferating. I began feeling a mild dissociation as a result of these prolonged feelings of unwellness. What was happening to me was too uncanny, defying logical explanation with every visit to the medical clinic. Was I suffering from an agent that had yet to be discovered? Was I going mad? Dark thoughts would flash before me like thunderbolts from an ash-ridden sky.

Of the many general practitioners who I frequented (and am still frequenting), only one took me seriously. The others all dismissed my claims as figments of a wild imagination or the tips of other underlying issues brewing in my subconscious. Some suggested I see a casework counselor or psychologist to help me unravel and cope. A psychiatrist solved my case by putting me on antidepressants and telling me that things would eventually work themselves out. Good one. The antidepressants weren't very user-friendly at all, destroying the lining in my stomach and wreaking havoc with my sex drive. Before I knew it, everything and everyone around me had transformed into a lively circus with clowns and props. One might call strong antidepressants "warped agents of amusement."

Since June 2008, I've been trying to piece together the remnants of my life again. I'm back at work and the gym, and I've begun writing again like never before. During the last few months, I've also taken some time to look deeper into the dilemma in which I find myself. Internet searches don't really bring up much. What scares me more than anything is that I can't find anything that remotely resembles my condition. The facts remain: I don't feel well within myself, yet medicine decrees I am perfectly healthy. It's a *wrongness* that is indeed very real, yet it eludes all forms of tangible definition. It's a juxtaposition with no logic or sense to it; yet it's the truth.

I am writing this author's note to you from the comfort of my writing desk, which overlooks a dramatic golf course. My field of vision is whitening, and my perception is distorted, though the strength to go on is there—alive and burning like never before. I've made up my mind to go to any lengths to find the answers I'm seeking. I am well prepared to search for them in alternative medicine, should Western methods fail to yield results; and the past sixteen years or so supports the hypothesis that none will eventuate. I guess when you feel your condition is gradually deteriorating, anything is worth a shot. Answers so often appear when questions have not yet been posed.

I will tell you that there are a few answers that have flowered in my being without having been sown by me. They come as a complete surprise, actually. One of them is a return to the old world, just like when I was a small child: the fervent belief in God, his archangels, and dimensions of existence above and below our own. Yes, I've done away with scientific inquiry for the time being. I need a break from it because, apart from not yielding answers, it's making me crazy.

I'm now a proud servant of God Almighty. That doesn't mean I'm going to dash to church and become an altar boy the first chance I get. Or that I'll attend Sunday confession and Holy Communion like I did when I was younger. That won't happen any time soon. What I'm inferring is that I'm deeply spiritual and profoundly aware of a cosmic consciousness that pervades and unites the universe and all entities within it. And because of this newfound religion, call it Neo-Platonic or Gnostic if you like, I've decided that it's time I finally open the floodgates of my soul so that you may see for yourself what sixteen years of coexistence with this ancient enemy has done to me.

Oh, and I've set up my own confessional booth in which to do it.

Remember those?

I've never, ever before confessed any of my demons on paper.

Until now, that is.

A confession

Is an admission of something,

At times tainted with a declaration of guilt,

At times without.


Did you attend confession at school?

Or when you felt you sinned?

Did the priest make you laugh

Or did you feel like you'd just

Scoffed down a truckload of chocolate

And were about to spew?


Fifty of my own are revealed in this book.


But whether or not

They're completely honest

Is another affair,

Isn't it?

*Prologue: A Time before This ...*

| | |
|---|---|
| BELIAL: | *Awake, oh, Proteus of all ill,* |
| | *The chaos-being; the demon,* |
| | *Who changes shapeless form at will* |
| | *And imperils all brave seamen.* |
| PROTEUS: | *I am here, Oh Captain of all dark,* |
| | *I hear your call to duty,* |
| | *This ship of pirates I'll embark* |
| | *To steal gold hearts and booty.* |
| BELIAL: | *Were you aware nine sons-of-might* |
| | *Now spread the Word by sea* |
| | *A ploy of heinous Aphrodite* |
| | *To hearten moral glee.* |
| PROTEUS: | *She hopes to stamp out your intent,* |
| | *Your yellowed filth and bile,* |
| | *Appealed and hoped I would repent,* |
| | *She thinks me so ductile.* |
| BELIAL: | *Take pus and semen from my vein,* |
| | *And call on our black ravens* |
| | *To splatter the most lethal strain* |
| | *Atop their Clay-Do havens.* |
| PROTEUS: | *My mind is null,* |
| | *My hands are bound,* |
| | *If death is what you wish for;* |
| | *I chose the heavens as my judge* |
| | *Twelve stars I called to witness,* |
| | *That should my silent dagger speak* |

*Against her best, her oldest,*

*I'd spare the bravest that she'd seek,*

*Her best beloved, her boldest.*

BELIAL: *Make of the clouds your flying steed,*

*Its reigns you'll weave*

*From shark bite,*

*Beseech the darkness not to cede*

*Oblivion to starlight.*

*Leave these mountains in your wake*

*And leap the hills; be active!*

*So hasten for your Father's sake*

*To bring that Simon captive.*

*He lives on Hickford Street, I know,*

*A house with thorny roses,*

*Make entrance from the duct below*

*At dusk when he reposes.*

*Please blend your seed into his spit,*

*Be shrewd in blood; be clever,*

*Then start to take him bit by bit,*

*And swallow him forever.*

*You'll find him in his bed tonight,*

*A child of twelve wee years,*

*With Mother Mary to his right,*

*Who keeps at bay his fears.*

PROTEUS: *I'll do exactly as you state*

*Unlike the rest who faulted.*

|            |                                          |
|------------|------------------------------------------|
|            | *Who went aloof-like through the gate*   |
|            | *And found the door well bolted.*        |
| BELIAL:    | *They dropped a rose there*              |
|            | *For a hook;*                            |
|            | *Their plans were not forsaken.*         |
|            | *They knocked until*                     |
|            | *The windows shook;*                     |
|            | *The brat did not awaken.*               |
| PROTEUS:   | *Fear not, I'll take that mortal man,*   |
|            | *I'll strike him mute and manic.*        |
|            | *I'll foil their God's eternal plan*     |
|            | *And roust all din and panic.*           |
| BELIAL:    | *Be sure to hunt for Solomon's key,*     |
|            | *Which sank in the Pelagic,*             |
|            | *They cure ailments by the threes*       |
|            | *Through sorcery and magic.*             |
| PROTEUS:   | *A world well void of human trace*       |
|            | *Is music to my ears,*                   |
|            | *Entrust the fiends of our own race*     |
|            | *To rouse their morbid fears.*           |

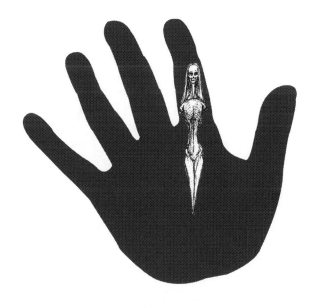

The Ancient Enemy

# Proteus

I am Apostolos:

He who has been sent

To preach of truth and ailments.

You ask how I might

Help a brother or sister?

This is a wonderful question,

For they are as unprepared as I

For what is to follow.

You shall not repeat

The forbidden knowledge

Disclosed on these pages.

It has long been lost.

I'm damned for telling you

Because it is against His wishes,

But it is my mission to deliver it.

I will tell you all that I know,

And you, brother or sister, will listen.


Sometime in late antiquity

The library of Alexandria burned.

With it burned an important manuscript,

*The Chronicle of Proteus*,

Which documented the work

Of an ancient enemy.

Don't ask me how I know;
Some things must not be questioned.


The ancient Greeks knew Proteus
As he who possessed the powers
Of foretelling the future
And of changing his shape at will.
He is viral and visceral at heart,
Quite literally with a mind of his own,
And a visual eye for creativity.
He doesn't wreak havoc with blood counts,
Nor can any ELISA or PCR test detect him—
Scientific inquiry still lags
Centuries behind his fiery footfalls.
Those who survive his screaming daggers
Parade as Pablo Picassos, Stephen Kings,
Zodiac killers, and even Jack the Rippers,
At times they hold a license
For split personality
And sometimes schizophrenia;
At other times they're the jaded junky
Chained by the leg in solitary solace
Or an affiliate of alcoholics anonymous
And self-help groups.


I am his sixteen-year-old vessel—

Last night he screwed me up the arse
So hard that my vision fucked up;
He impeded my short-term memory,
Making the bedroom walls appear bestial,
And illustrated images
On the television screen
Inside my dirty hard drive
Were not interpreted
As 3-D animation cartoon clips
Of rip-off-rhetoric spiritualist
Sylvia Browne
Because they lacked
Sense and sensibility.
I became sensibly stuck
In this synaptic transmission labyrinth
Of chemical and electrical back and forth,
Panicking and heaving for breath
Between artificially constructed ideals
Of Utopia and eternal Emptiness.

Then Pandora's paroxysms blew up in my face
Because he appointed pendulums
And my dead great-grandfather
For spiritual supervision
And advised on how to stamp
The pointless past under my feet;

Coerced me to play peeping Tom

With the thirteen-year-old girl

Near the graveyard

And then checked out how good

My goliath cock looked in the mirror.

He had impure thoughts on ice

About bending me over for a bull

Like perverted Pasiphae

And then whispered that I should

Write notorious novels about it

When nobody was listening.


I know he will not leave me.

At times he breeds with such force

That I am turned inside out

And upside down,

And the only certainty I experience

Is that of known uncertainty.

In this light, the world,

Together with its people,

Its ideals, strivings, sufferings, and passions

Are not real.

They are imaginary, illusory even.

The moment then passes,

But a small seed of truth has been sown.

It grows according to the quaky ground

Which seems to see-saw in his favor

When time rams the foot down

On the adjacent accelerator.


Why would I so desire Panacea

When I am Proteus's felt-tip pen?

She'll never unload

Into my psychic world

The way he plots with much panache.

# A stroke of wrongness

Something is very wrong.
I do not feel well
Sitting on the throne of my being.
It has begun feeding
From my spiritual arteries.
It has begun to set loose
This restlessness inside of me.

The light seems so much farther,
The earth much less nurturing.
The water has lost potency
In quenching my thirst.

Like the Meltemi wind,
It has uplifted trivial, everyday matters
And left behind
Only the desire
To understand.

# Secret

There's this young man
Who has now ceased
To wake upon
The cock's lively crow at sunrise.

There's this crystalline clock
Beside his desk
That has begun to recount
The same seconds, minutes, and hours,
All swathed in bubbles of inertia.

There's this broken record
Called his *heart*
That pleads with the same mechanical words
Of experience and truth, over and over,
Which no real voice of science will heed.

There's this thorny seed
That latched itself deep inside him long ago,
Flowering the same brackish petals of darkness
That refuse to find expression
In the light of modern medicine.

There's this stack

Of dreams and aspirations

In his suburban bedroom

That are now buried beneath the growing weight

Of daytime demons,

Made of burning limbs and rotting flesh.


There's a certain traveler

Slouched over the green and crème railings

Of his verandah outside,

Crying with the eyes

Of those who've been unjustly cast

Twice a stranger

In a life formerly their own.

# Three degrees of unwellness

There are three degrees of unwellness
In this waiting room.

The unlucky teenager wheels herself around
Without any feeling in her legs.
The gay guy doesn't feel well
Within himself
And, like her, half dead
In a queer kind of way—
Pardon the pun.

Which of the two is worse off?
Maybe the old hag
With a mouse on her shoulder
And the rat traps
Down the old corridor
Suffering from a chronic
Paraplegia of the soul.

# Formulaic medicine

You wear your spectacles,

Your white lab coat,

Your polished intelligence—

All those years of formulaic thinking

Which speak the brash tongue of hard science,

And all those medical texts around your room

That serve to intimidate

And scream treason against those

Who dare to object to their undisputed truth—

And, with an assumed omniscience

That offends the gods themselves,

Take a look at some test results

And then pass judgment

Upon my testimonial of suffering prematurely,

Without comprehending

That your hard-earned knowledge

And experience

Might someday turn against you,

Unless you heed to the facts

And physics of one's heart.

# The subjectivity of experience

You say
Objectivity is defined
By empirical evidence
And all other symptoms
Fall into the category
Of subjective experience.

I say
It is easy to pigeonhole
All else
As subjective
When you are not the one
Rotting in your own body.

# Diagnosis X

They don't like to admit defeat

Because it punches throbbing holes

In their medical hologram of the universe.

There's nothing wrong with you,

Except in that bent, little mind of yours.

That's what they tell you

When they don't understand.

Or simply when the answer eludes them.

And if they repeat it enough times,

They might convince you to believe it.

And if you believe, it may actually come to pass.

And if it doesn't come to pass,

They'll just put you on Effexor,

Flex their brainy muscles,

Wave flags of sovereignty,

And tell you to see a psychiatrist

'Cause "it's all for the best."

# Unanimous verdict

With those golden locks
Draped over your forehead,
Those merciful eyes
That wept with viscous empathy,
You gently blushed before
A moment's pause
On the last frontier of defeat
And asked me,
"If worst comes to worst,
Is this something you can live with?"

And trembling in the revelation
Of a sluggish death sentence
I dropped to my knees and told you,
"Ask the one-legged egret
By the muddy river
And the cyclist
Paralyzed by a truckie
High on smack last night.
Ask the evergreen
Slowly yellowed by sulfuric acid
And the worthy trophy
Rusted by timely dampness on my shelf.
Ask the bony sea cave

Gnawed at by the incoming tides

And the rape victim

Who cries herself to sleep at night.


Ask and let their unanimous verdict

Echo from the unspoken grottos of the earth—

That joint choir of laments, muddy anguish,

And fear with no detectable bottom,

And of all emotion that must never be known."

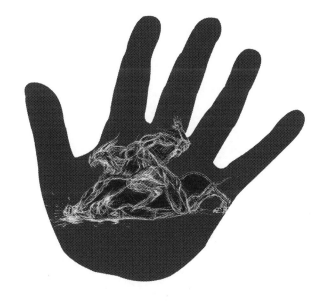

Behold my Wrath

# Tombstone

*What has been will be*;
For there is nothing new under the sun.


When I die I shall be
Buried beside my beloved,
Deserted to the ravages of wind and water—
Time shall cease smiling
Upon me and forget my sepulcher.
My children's hands shall no longer
Lay violets and roses to pacify oblivion,
Blind and stern-faced.
My lachrymatory shall be dismissed
From hauling around weighted memories,
Eulogies of grief, and then
Be spat upon by buoyant rainwater.
I know my final resting place
Shall inevitably be perturbed
And my very dust sifted
In search of gainful trinkets,
Or be switched with another brother's,
Or be leveled for the sake
Of self-importance—the self-esteem
Of humanity's living ego.

*What has been will be*;
For there is nothing new under the stars.


Everything shall bow to the inevitable

Fate of ruin and forgetfulness some day,

Just like the silent echo of our eventful past.

My only wish is for the grievance

I knew in life to be righted

By the assurance of its dormancy in death.

And may the cupola of the sky tumble,

The earth spew its insides out,

And the order of the universe be overturned

If ever my eternal rumination is disturbed.

# Holidays

We organize a formal catch-up once a month.

How exciting, hey?

Don't you find it so amusing

That we sit with our hands crossed

And have nothing more to say

Other than what transpired on our holidays

And how crap the Melbourne weather

Has been as of late?


And after we stuff ourselves, it's all about you.

You claim that your cutesy smile

And mermaid figure

Have knocked down hordes of gorgeous men.

You're proud of being

A first-class metrosexual magnet,

But I can see beneath

That PVC spacesuit

To the Martian child

Begging for acceptance,

Quivering and insecure about

Her big mouth

And beady eyes—for that you can be sure.


We both agree

That holidays are soul music

Amidst the silence of monotonous routine,

But that's it as far

As common denomination will go.


Mine are made of turquoise silk,

Of Enya, Mozart, and exotic Oriental music,

Of fiery volcanoes and forbidden mountains,

And of Elysian roads far less traveled.

But yours are of that cheap, red, polyester sort,

Of pop and trance, of petrol-sniffing raves

And drug-infested beach parties

On Myconos and Ibiza,

And of an underground Hades,

Whose darkness has raped and murdered

Millions of Persephones like you.

# The physician

You told the patient

That there was nothing wrong,

Except in his mind,

And then went home

To enjoy a candlelit dinner for two.


Six months later,

You were sorry that the patient

Had died from virulent cancer ...


... And then went home

To enjoy a candlelit dinner for two.

# Treasure hunt

Just look at you,

Typical candidate of vain glory.

Stop looking for the tomb of Christ

And Turin shrouds

And that precious Holy Grail,

You stupid archeologist.

Your peers go on fools' quests for Aztec tombs,

Inca gold, and those seven cities of gold.

Do you really think you'll end up

With money brimming from your pockets,

A nice girl by your side,

That Ferrari you've always wanted,

And your pretty-boy face

Shining like a million bucks

On the history channel.

Do you expect them to painstakingly document

The life of the orphaned child

Who came from nowhere

To become a global-superstar crap?


There's some fungal megalomania

Growing in your cerebral cortex;

Don't get too ahead of yourself.

Your strings are being pulled

By significant others,

And you'll only ever shine

For as long as the brain police so desire!


It seems fantasy is nothing

But a guilty pleasure,

So somebody has got to stop

That hero virus with its fedora and bullwhip

From replicating

Because Robert Langdon and Indiana Jones

Can only dodge cops and solve riddles

In pop-fiction flicks.

Don't you dare believe a word

They hand-feed you in the media

About the truth of it all, boy!


Just ask poor Howard Carter

If it's all lovey-dovey

Or if he ended up with Sophie Neveu

And a piece of mind

After he set loose Pandora's Box in 1922.

And while we're on the subject

Of post-Tutankhamun,

Would you please stop to think

Why those prissy, necrophile Egyptians

Would have buried their dead

As if a tornado from Texas

Had just been through?

While we're on the subject

Of archeological enigmas,

Why would the *Prince of the Lilies*

Be wearing a headdress

Reserved for a priestess?

Trust Sir Arthur Evans

To shed truth on that?

We might not need satellite images

Or X-rays of Lord Elgin's intentions

To see through to his bony

"It-was-for-the-best" excuse

When he took his balls back to England.


If that's not enough ambiguity for you,

We've now got Modern-day Atlanteans

In the mix, trying to flavor every discovery

With a pang of new-age spiritual crap.

And if it's not that,

It's psychic astrologers

Recalling Lemuria

And the lost, telepathic abilities

Of its womenfolk.

No, sweetie, you won't find Atlantis in Antarctica

With those phony Mohammedan maps,

But there might be many Dorothy Eadys

Remembering past lives

Bedding pharaohs or princesses

Trapped in some citadel

If it gets them some attention

At the hair salon next week

Or perhaps a few minutes of fame

On the Oprah Winfrey Show.


I believe the Freemasons and secret societies

Know as much about the meaning of life

As Chinese rug peddlers know

About quadratic equations.

And with Anna Hedges

Convincing herself of the legitimacy

Of her own big, fat, Greek lies

You too might be tempted to find

Your own crystal skulls

Under collapsed alters in a temple

And then visit a psych ward to get over

The guilty conscience of it all.


Truly, why might you all be looking for,

Charts and maps that will reveal hidden treasure?

Is it really about self-worth?

Achievement, maybe?

I guess everybody's looking for something

Although only a tosser wouldn't know

There's no real value in matter

No matter how old!


I believe one day you might just wake

To a different angle of what you're seeking,

Which are meaningful patterns

In this consciousness hologram of virtual reality,

Which we all agree is the cosmos defined.

# Who framed Natasha, the dispenser?

The stumpy dispenser is wilting
In one of the counseling rooms next door,
Battered by heroin addicts,
Vandalized by the homeless,
Used by those frequented
By Archangel Gabriel
And handed the rose of Immaculate Deception,
Spat at by the sexually abused
And those hit by broomsticks,
Stabbed in the neck with syringes
And pimped in the parking lot
For a whiff of speed.

They abuse her with threats
After jamming a dollar or two
Down her stinking slots
To absorb their shock factor
Like an airhead full of psychobabble.

She then pumps out cans of Coke
And packets of Fantails
From a calculating crack to distract them,
But when the going gets tough
She'll suddenly short-circuit

So that her mental electricity won't skyrocket

And prompt AGL to issue an infringement notice

Stamped PRIVATE and CONFIDENTIAL,

Enlightening that she's been framed

For stealing pennies full of thought

Without dispensing atonement

Because she's always out of order.

# Predictions from the Bureau of Unrequited Love

Your chirpy voice
Asks me through
The telephone receiver
What the day
Might bring tomorrow,
And I must confess
The forecast is
Dependent entirely
Upon your actions.

Expect a top
Of thirty-two degrees Fahrenheit
With a strong, southwesterly wind
Of thirty knots
And teary hailstorms
If you forget to send
My AIDS cycle T-shirt
In the post again.
Possible thunder and lightning
And a developing low-pressure system
Of cumulonimbus giants
Outside your doorstep
If you don't call me

On my twenty-ninth birthday.

And sunny California

To be separated from

The mainland by fits of righteous fury

If your apathy doesn't stop

Loitering around my side-streets

Like morning fog,

Undaunted.


I suppose

Twenty-four hours

Of unrequited love

Can be more eventful

Than one full year

Of reciprocal affection.

# Black cobra

I startled a black cobra
While hiking through the desert
On a glorious, Wednesday afternoon.

Instead of striking me
With her freckly fangs,
She dashed for the nearest rock
And buried her head under it,
Unaware that her limbless torso
Was still showing.

My mother once told me
That all serpents have
An uncanny ability
To either ambush their prey
Or wedge themselves under rocks.
I presume they're not nearly
As good at hiding
As they are
At delivering their lethal bite—
But utterly powerless
And even pitiful
Once you've yanked them
By the neck.

# The Stud on the train

I gather beauty is a bigot,
With VIP privileges,
And always guilty of discrimination.


You see that metrosexual over there?
He's a beauty, no doubt;
Brad Pitt, eat your heart out.
The *Men's Health* magazine would pay tons
To plaster his face all over their covers.


He's prim and proper
And might have just brought his suit
From a city department store.
Jesus Christ!
He's looking at me with that casual,
"I-know-I'm-hot–and-can-have-you-if-I-want" look.
His muscles bulge like big oranges
When he moves his arms.
They look ready to split
A shirt two sizes too small.
He's either wearing a black jockstrap
Or a G-string;
His lips glisten
With an unnatural tinge of pink.

No doubt he must be very proud

Of his "cancer" job at the local solarium,

But why he won't bend over

To pick up a newspaper

That's just been knocked out of a woman's lap

By a junkie is beyond me.

Perhaps he doesn't want it to crease pants

Which dig deep into his ass crack.

Or because he's really

Just a softie—

A pop princess inside.


This is one manufactured Ken doll

That Hollywood would embrace

As long as he wears suspenders

And garter belts after midnight,

Carries pink and purple condoms in his jackets,

And gets fucked up the ass

By the manager of some big studio.

*Actions and Reactions*

# Mercy

Have mercy
Upon me, Lord,
For no amount
Of faults
Deserves a punishment
That is this
Time-battered vessel
I reside in.

# *What's in a name?*

My mind can no longer rest at midnight.

With two pewter hands and a green orb,

I lie awake,

Breaking free of squares and syllogisms,

Transcending the hypotenuse

Of right-angled triangles.

Passing from one dimension into another,

From the first to the second,

The third to the fourth and back again,

To compromise a microscopic assailant within,

Invisible and bio-phobic,

The hater of fortitude

That cringes at every utterance of my name.

# Shooting Star

When a little spark from the night sky

Plummets from the canopy of stars above,

Somewhere, someplace,

A being of light has been born.

So make certain you light a candle,

And make a heartfelt wish

That it never be touched by the darkness

Of what it's like to feel completely alone

In a world void

Of both heartfelt light and heaven.

# In the psychiatrist's chair

When I lie slumped
In your retractable chair on Monday nights,
You pull the silver cord out of my head
And pick apart the perverted anatomy
Of my unconscious mind
To see how it works.

You give me permission to relax
Amongst bubbles of fine, white light
On the beaches of Hawaii, Port Douglas,
And even the lagoons of distant Crete—
To escape from chronic worry
To escape the four corners of home,
Which have become saturated in cockroaches.

But when I'm not looking,
You drop ghost desires and attractions
And tacky bits of aphrodisiac
Between its folds,
Ones that have gone undetected by the MRI.
And when you finally breathe
My wondering soul back into the resting clay,
I awake, feeling like the living dead.

You say that many lives ago

I was a horny vampire,

Tonguing your motherly breasts,

Drawing blood from your jugular vein

With a hard bite,

And tasting that fifty-year-old Celtic pussy

Aching to be filled by a Zorba freight train

Of burning seed.

# The language of dreams

Standing beside me in the darkness,
The Old Ones squeezed my hand
And told me that nothing in the sky
Is exactly what it seems—

Kesar's legions dropped their spears
On the floor of heaven
At the call of Buddha,
And the stars are but sharp reflections,
Smiling through the holes.

Then they slipped into
Their silent caverns underground
And promised they would awaken
When the world remembered.

# The Traveler

This passing traveler
Stopped by for the night,
Dressed in splendid armor;
A most chivalrous knight.

He was swift in causing me
To remember my true name
He said, "Seek and search out your answers,
But only in fair game."

Then he went to salvage
Other hopeless dreamers.

# Friend or foe

We can't pick our family,
But we have the luxury
Of picking our friends and lovers,
Many of whom are subliminally woven
Into cobwebs of more sinister motives.

You say that I'm a close pal and ally,
But would that opinion change
If you knew you're merely
The stone-cobbled bridge
To the greener side of the river?

# Soul mates

I've sent you a glorious rosebud,
One that emerged from the African wilderness;
The most scarlet, robust, the plumpest of all,
Its snowy lips leave me panting for breath;
Its sweaty scent chars my loins like lava.
Fine-stemmed and lean,
It roared through Hades
And into the land of the living;
Like a blond lion,
It came forth from amidst
An entangled web of toxic leaves;
A bolt of aching love
In the milky sea of unlikelihood—
And thou didst give light to my soul
Till then wrapped in darkness.

# The little ones that spring forth

The little ones that spring forth
Are the flesh of future gods,
Quite unlike this outdated holy bread
Dipped in cheap house wine
From the local supermarket.

Take two and swallow,
Sit back, relax,
And enjoy the mental wholeness of it all
Without telling Isis
That you've ripped off
Her Black Veil of mourning.
She doesn't need to know
We're in the monocular-vision theatre
Or that we're hearing colors and seeing voices—
Otherwise she'd thwack us on the head
With a bouquet of flowers
That's really a horse-drawn chariot
By candlelight.

Check out the walls of the house:
They've been blown to smithereens.
So just let yourself slip into something
More comfortable, dissolve,

Like a Berocca tablet,

In the pool of primordial-glass water

And be catapulted over

The National parks of Whittlesea Shire

Into the forested Grampians

That rise, tier above tier, into heaven;

Fly me to the moon with leonine paws

And kaleidoscopic vision

Minus the romance hogwash,

Touch its bony surface

And bounce back into a room

Of liquid mercury

With giant bumblebees

Smashing against the windows,

Faces and limbs suspended

From the gelatinizing mass

And hanging above me

Like giant snots.


Eagle-headed, the living

Deader-than-shit

And recycled dead from Hades

Climb out of the walls,

Dance around me

With faces that peel open

To reveal skulls that check me out,

And ask whether I take
My coffee with cream
Or if I prefer jam or honey
On my burnt toast.

Then they try to shove
Their prehensile penises
That have small jaws and eyes
Down my sore throat,
Their blistered skin weeping
Yummy blue battery acid
And electronic vocals that make
Me cum like Krakatoa.

In the aftermath of a Vitamin C tsunami,
I pull the telephone cord from the plug
So I can stop tasting data
Of archetypes and Platonic ideas
Because it's not so good for my health,
But the dark still pokes me
With its invisible hands.

I scream and scream,
And nobody will believe me
When I tell them
What it's like for a blind man
To finally see without seeing

And come to grips

With spiritual madness,

Which will be

The mainstream common sense

And ruin of the world some day.

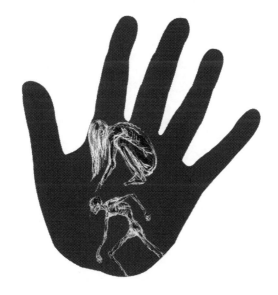

*In the Aftermath*

# The beast within

You tell me
That I should not fear
The darkness within.

I tell you
That I am not afraid
Of the darkness within—

Simply because
I've never felt
The light to begin with.

# Music of the mind

The mind itself
Can no more
Cure an ailment
Than the music
Of Mozart or Tchaikovsky
Can stop a cunning blade
From drawing blood.

The mind
Numbs itself
With a few glasses of Tequila
And hopes the chords
Of *Moonlight Sonata*
Shed some light on remission.

# Jesus loves me

"Jesus loves me, this I know,
For the Bible tells me so."

Does one really need
A discourse to validate
That he is loved by his savior?

Love cannot be told.
It must be felt with a thorny heart.

# Love at first sight

How do I prove that I am worthy?

How do I impress with only simple words?

How do I show that I know how to love?

Once in a while, an outcast

Is wrongfully accused of being a madman.

Time then forgives, and he is cast a mastermind.

# The gift of observation

What is he writing over there,
That young man with a notebook?

Is it the seed of a poem or novel?
Is it scraps of a new syllogism or enigma?

He might be delving into the mind
Of the cripple next door.
He might be imaging life as a giant sequoia.
He might be exalting the sun, the moon,
Or even the starry firmament.
Or perhaps stringing together
Not-so-sincere complements
To woo his lovers.

He might even be writing about you,
Who stares at him for hours on end
Through a slit in your curtain.

# Astrological dilemmas

Why seek your answers in all the wrong places?
Why insist that fate is circumscribed
By the busy highway of stars?
Why bother looking for portents
In the heavenly bodies?

Looking at the night sky
Is unlike scrying a crystal ball.
You only ever get glimpses
Of what your life was like
Some light years ago.

# Time the merciless

Nightfall has come—yet again.

From my window, I can see
The city speckled with streetlights
And the shriek of a passing airplane overhead.

A deep hush resettling into loud spaces
Like a sheet of fine dust
Is disturbed only by the hum of a refrigerator.
Thankfully, a leaking tap in the kitchen
Has given the primordial night
Some discernible rhythm.
The ticking clock by my side
Even sparks a beat
In its monotonous vocals.

They, as well as I, have aged together.
I guess as creatures of the dark and abandon,
We're all content with measuring
The only thing left after you
—Splinters of time—

# Near the edge

I suppose the loss of my padded armor
Might have something to do
With breaking out in hoots of laughter
In solemn waiting rooms,
Deserting one mundane task for another,
Ignoring the mandatory routines of the day,
Walking the same network of concentric circles
Upon wakefulness; redrawing them the next day
And thinking about how far I can shoot my load
Across the room and up your arse some.

Surely they are but necessary adjustments
Of aberrant change in my crabby shell
If I am to keep myself from cartwheeling
Into the netherworld of pentagrams
And colored circuses of fine, white dust?

# Entity creation

You plead guilty to the Holy One

That your own Self was long ago supplanted

By an entity that could not resist

The urge to sink its mischievous teeth—

When no one was looking—into the golden apple

Hanging from the branch of a neighbor's tree.


I, my friend, have often felt the same.

No one ever believes me, though—

Not even my neighbor.

# Egregore

There's this tiny egregore
Living in a small statue within my room
Casting my shadow upon the burning asphalt,
He has your eyes and smile.
The same stars hang from his crown.
The same words seep from his tongue.
He makes love the way you do.
He dispels doubts that are untrue.

Don't think he's just a casual part
Of my life,
Coloring the time
With handcuffs and whips,
Loud kisses, and quaky orgasms

That small dab of laughter in the dark.

# Have faith in the silent footfalls of love

Don't mind
The Divine Physician,
Quietly tiptoeing
Amongst the crying sufferers
In hospital wards.
There's much to be done
Around their stale walls:
Ailments to cure with light,
Wounds to dress with his Word,
Pain to soothe with love.
He's there,
As real as the oxygen
We breathe into our lungs;
Ready to blow fresh
Air into their lives
If only they just believed.

# Ozone

Listen!

Can you hear it?

It whistles through door cracks,

Screams through ravines,

And rustles the branches of the giant cypresses

Like some paranoid schizophrenic.

Can you hear it? It's getting louder.

Like blood, it pumps through Mama Pasha's

Fleshy limbs and animates her.

It is slow and rhythmic, a relaxed breathing

That will sustain her womb and offspring.

Pause just for a moment and hear it.

It is unsoiled in spirit and force; so pure.

It is everywhere,

Yet absent from our narrow minds;

It is the noisy future; a miracle waiting to enter

Our consciousness in a few years from now,

Or perhaps in 2012 when the forked tongue

Of our wrinkled sun, Tonaihtuh, is severed

By a silent knife held by this Other.

Can you hear it?

I've become drunk on faith just thinking

About its brilliance and an outside chance

for a cure ...

*Myths and Ruminations*

# Mythology

The eyes see what they want to see.
Is it a thunderbolt or the voice of fury?
The wind or a fleeting nymph?


The mind, too, sees what it wants to see.
Is Psyche and Cupid a love story
Or the plight of one's soul to find true love?
Is Pygmalion and Galatea
About prejudice, subjugated by love,
Or a misogynist punished by the gods for his sin,
Or is it about fetishes and necrophilia?


The bubbly magic of it all
Is that it can be either one of these,
Or neither, or both.
Once the three-dimensional spell is broken,
Eyes might not be worth having;
The mind not worth believing in.

# Narcissus and his girls

Have you heard a myth
About a Greek man—Narcissus?
All the girls who laid eyes on him
Longed to be his,
But he was so wrapped up in himself
He fell in love with
His own reflection by a rock pool
And drowned trying to hone in for a closer look.

All of us, at some stage or another,
Have been guilty of such vanity.
Not the beautiful, though.

# The poet and the priest

When a poet and a priest
Fell on their knees before Odysseus
And begged to be spared,
The righteous hero
Thrust the murderous knife
Into the priest
Without a second thought.

And I ask you,
Is the chronicler of God's life
Worth that much more
Than the enforcer of His will?

Odysseus might have felt awe
To slay a man who'd been taught
His divine craft by God.
But spare a timely thought
For the priest as well,
Who dedicates his entire life
Trying to advocate it.

# Midas

I don't know if you know,
But there are grains of gold
In the sands of the river Pactolus in Turkey,
So my grandmother tells me.

Do you know Midas, Grandson?
He was king of Phrygia, the land of roses.
One day he wished for gold and got it.
He also preferred Pan's pipes of hashish
To Apollo's flowery lyre.
Stupidity, unlike roses, gets around.
Just ask the magic mushrooms
By the riverbed; they'd tell you.

Be wary of what you wish for
When you bathe in its waters, my child,
For no gold can come good of wishing
If it is barren of common sense.

# The book's curse

*Isaac*

Is the name

I cherish most

Because in it

Lives all

I've ever had,

Or wanted,

Or been.


If it perishes

From the leaf

Of this wordy tomb,

Then yours shall

Be written onto

A clay figurine,

Tufts of its hair

Bound with evil curses

And then smashed

Into a million

Or so pieces.

# Sooner or later

You are Alive.

You are Awareness.

You are Awakening Consciousness
Making sense of the words on this page.
Your neurons establish patterns
Of labyrinthine pathways through which
Chemical and electrical impulses fire,
Igniting past and future,
Experience and emotion,
Speech and thoughts,
And sometimes a thing or two about
Righteousness and common sense.

You are Alertness
Fluttering in the wind like a candle flame,
Flickering out only when the gust picks up.
Sooner or later, somebody comes along
With the power to reignite it.

Your Awakening Conscience, that is.

# The island of silence

The stone giants
Of worlds before our own
Remain animate only as long
As the sculptors
Who carved them
Live to transliterate
Their thoughts and feelings.

Once they're gone,
Neither their sons,
Grandsons, or great-grandsons
Have the talent
To interpret
The revelations
Of a silent language.

# Love myth

You ask if love is real

Or is it just the *stuff*

Of Linda Howard novels,

Of Shakespeare's *Romeo and Juliet,*

And sentimental Hollywood flicks like *Titanic?*


"I couldn't tell you," I blush.

"I'm a stranger to that *stuff* myself.

Ask the bald eagle perched

On its nest high up in the mountains.

Ask the little finger

Pointing to the moon at night."

# Supernatural

What lies behind
Those piercing blue eyes
Is a socially acceptable
Form of madness,
Apparent only
To the like-minded few.

You try to make sense
Of the immediate future
By asking spirits of the light
To spell out messages
On Ouija boards
And tarot-card readings
Customized to fit
Your own slanted wishes
With never a thought about willpower—

Hoping for a truthful answer
But unwilling to be it;
Seeking a clear-cut direction
But unwilling to pave it;
Screening unintelligible notes for logic
But far too busy to find it in your own life.

All the meaning and purpose

That one is entitled to by right of birth

Are there; tangible and full of song

And ready to be taken by the horns

Without invocations or evocations—

If only you weren't so insecure.

j k l m n o p q r s
i t
h u
g v
f w
e d c b a z y x

yes    no

1234567890

Good Bye

The Savage Past

# A dream of the past

Dedicated to Omm Sety (1904–1982)

Was it all wishful thinking?

Was it a false memory

Implanted with my fervent yet small hands

That wanted so much to believe?

Was it a dream that kept stumbling,

Again and again,

Over the same sequence?

Or was it the lifting of a veil

That had been hanging over my teary eyes

For as long as I can remember?


For how long

Must I go on remembering

All those French kisses;

The pink shirt tossed over the bed,

Still throbbing with your springtime pheromones;

Your disarming laughter

And crummy bits of an undeciphered script

About thinking with our hearts?


Perhaps for not a second more;

Perhaps for all eternity.

# Sweetheart, just let yourself be

Sweetheart, why won't you
Just let yourself just *be*?
There is much life within *be* to be had.

Why must you ruin our momentous moment?
One which lies under a little black bridge,
Breathless with deep bruises on the nape
Of our necks and a trail of wet kisses
And snail trails that have left our baby makers
Without the visible signs of ache or pulse.


The bridge casts shadows onto our forms
And then carves lasting impressions
Of it all in our minds' eyes,
Deep in the spring afternoon, shielding us from
Rays that threaten to blow our cover
From the nosy air spirits
That won't stop bitch-slapping the corn
And gossiping about the pillow man
With a hard pole up his arse.
Time is somewhat ignorant too—
It has not yet noted the *be* to be had.
Or the *beings* that thought it—those heretics!
Or the stains on my jocks
As we walk back to car, for that matter.

But please don't look past the clapping corn
To the next guy down.
Don't you dare peer over your shoulder
To see if your sinister intentions
Took root in spring.
Not a glance toward the bleeding horizon
That aids and abets all
That cannot and must not be known.

I fear the Western limit so much because
It makes plans, plans, and more plans;
It moves two steps forward, three to the side,
And one giant leap back again.
Yes, it's a right-angled triangle that it's traced
To coerce you into bettering yourself
Through words and numbers—
Carefully educated guesses strung together
By natural selection to form Darwinian theories
In support of genetic freaks, fast-food living
And the nano-robotic intelligence in you.

I know that it keeps asking you to ponder
Stupid questions about your future,
About whom you are
And what you want from this life,

About your loved ones, your identity.

Why must you aspire and dream and hope

For the toys which the selfish brat in you deems

Necessary today but won't give a rat's arse about

In a few years from now

Or once you've acquired them?

Nothing lasts forever, right?

You're the one who told me so.


Trust me when I tell you

To huddle near that Cypress tree over there

And look the tree's spirit in the eyes.

Once the Gorgon inside

Has spirited you down to stone,

Begin to comprehend

How your next-door neighbors

All sweat blood and tears to make a buck or two.

Comprehend how the leash around their neck

Strings tighter and tighter

With every bird nest they build,

With every emotional past they sew.


Like highway bull ants travelling

At about a million light years per second,

They try hard to carve

Their own meaningful fates

Out of papier-mâché,

Pondering the mathematical probabilities

Of success or failure before the harsh

Critic and judge within themselves

Points the finger to remind of solemn promises—

Those of salvation or eternal damnation.

Now, how the hell

Can you expect

Stones, bridges, or even corn

And the everlasting mountains of the West

To remember you long after your hourglass

Runs short with an attitude like that?

# Alexander's mantle

I can't remember how long ago now,
But little pink elephants danced on the bed lamp,
Donald and Mickey wouldn't chat
Because they were too busy
Squabbling about the curtains,
And the mean lady next door
Did hocus-pocus stuff when it rained.

Back then he was just a short,
Stumpy, Greek bossy-boots
With blond curls and a short skirt,
Whom little kids from the East
Called "*Iskandar*," the "Boogeyman."
And they had to stay inside,
Otherwise they would have to learn
The Zorba dance,
Eat Greek feta cheese,
And have tzatziki breath
All day long.
Eww!

I would sometimes be so scared
To turn the page in the dimmed light
Because I'd have to go horsy riding

Away from Greece to places

Where people spoke funny

And wrapped toilet paper around dead bodies,

Where men painted their faces like girls

And mountain bears danced around campfires.

By the end of the night,

I'd be scared and want to go home.


Then I'd lie still and vigilant

If the sleep fairy forgot to visit,

Guarding your mantle with my baby face,

My small hands wrapped tightly around

My magical reading carpet,

And stuffed, silly Kharagöz

Would make me giggle by saying

I'd grow up to be a man like you someday.

# Demogorgon

The old world has been shattered
As I am no longer the one at the end
Of the umbilical cord.
The new world is unjust.
Justice and faith lie in the marrow
Of my bones no more.

I am the Fallen One, a child of my time,
A dominion of the past.
I have disobeyed humanity's conscience
And strung on my Destroyer top,
Poured chlorine onto carpet and parquetry,
Hot water onto the mattresses.
The bedrooms look like Sumatra
After it was hit by armed tidal forces.
I spin round and round
Like an out-of-control merry-go-round,
Squirting Morning Fresh onto family portraits
And Natuzzi furniture,
And then curl up in the sinister wardrobe
To gnaw my teeth in fetal position
Whilst dismantling Vaultron
In fits of laughter and accomplishment.

The darkness squeezes my temples,

And I roar with grief,

Watering my dog pen

And drawing boiling blood from my furry face

To relieve it from pressurized psychopathy,

Revenge reactions, absence of attention,

Temperature, and then drink

Chocolate Big M to dull severe

Toothache caused by cavities

No longer filled by the enamel

Of unconditional love.


The world I inhabit today

Is continually being destroyed.

I wish lopsidedly for a newer one still.

Justice and faith lie

In the marrow of my bones no more.

I seethe in silence

And sometimes in sympathy

At all conscious awareness.

# Let the reigns of your heart free

All my joy is a pale reflection
In this little stitch work of green frills,
Messy blue hair, and a porcelain expression
That screams "Ain't misbehavin'!"
Cheeky splendor that puts
Any little goody-goody china doll to shame.

Patches of my childish funland
Hang from his checkered outfit,
Like angel's hair from Santa's arctic grotto.
His geometric patterns are a breath of fresh air
Wafting over my cluttered desk
Of mundane writing tasks.
He tells me that the past has not been unkind;
Nothing much has changed
In the last twenty-nine years.

The small expeditions around the neighborhood
With my battered tricycle,
The door-knocking, egg-throwing,
And water-balloon fighting
That unraveled in the deep hours of the night
Still dangle from the sleeves
Of an Armani suit I bought last week.

The days of playing dress up
And pretend are well and truly alive—
Just less tangible
As I don't wear sluttish lipstick,
Mum's silver nightgown
And clear nail polish anymore.

My red-nosed buddy stares back at me
With a sense of playfulness in the dim light,
Inviting me with his silent grin
To join that lovey-dovey circus again;
His titillating colors pleading me
To let the reigns of my heart free
With such urgency, he could almost be real.

# Healing in motion

Young love is bare-chested and barefoot,
Wearing red boardies, no underwear,
And trampling over hot stones.
She's lively, unrelenting.
She knows exactly what she wants.

"Cum! Cum!" her lover tells her.
"Cum now!" she screams.
"I'd rather die
Than give you power over me," he says.
She stops blowing him.
"But I give you power over me!"
Her body, her smile,
Her ambition, have all vanished.
There is only her voice left to her—
The echo that can follow but not speak;
The echo that has the last word
But no power to speak first—
That's how it's always been.

The unconscious, just like an assailant,

Always returns to the scene of a crime

And relives it.

Then it drinks of forgiveness

And heals.

# Ever after

In the beginning,
Or maybe somewhere left of the middle,
The Holy Spirit hovered over
The primordial waters,
Seeking his other half.

He saw it when he peered down—
The same burning eyes,
The same priestly hair,
Even the same blemishes
Around the forehead.

He found himself loving this other half
Beyond human comprehension.
In fact, he'd dreamt of loving it
Years before his thoughts
Ever had the chance
To stumble across any meaning
In its cosmic beauty.

But every attempt to coerce it,
To leave the amatory of the frothy ocean
And inhabit every living cell in his body
Was answered with light impressions,

Vague echoes, and mindless deflections
During the day
And phlegmatic yawns at night.

Something wasn't right.
He was Eolian and alive.
His other half abyssal,
Cold, calculating, and illusory even.
He was hot and urgent like the Etesian.
His other half ruminated like doldrums.
He loved.
His other half cared not for meaning,
Reason, nor salvation.
His own sobs skidded along
The surface of the sea.
His other half just absorbed.

The bio-phosphorescence of the sea
Knew what had gone wrong,
But the little seagulls he asked for help
Couldn't shed any light on the mystery.

Once he became
Dejected with the cosmos,
Which had proven itself
An abomination,

He sunk it

Back into the alphabet soup,

Deeper and deeper

Into an asthenosphere of chaos.


Even though the timely dissolution

Of trauma and injustice

Left no trace of the lithospheric experiment

As having occurred,

Remnants of Paleozoic love

Did become fossilized somewhere

Deep in the Christ part of him—

The only part that encompassed

A likelihood of having any ever after.

# Last thoughts of a sailor's life

According to the art of divination
I am an old soul—my shells corrode,
My noses end up battered like the sphinx's,
But my essence ploughs on through the ages.

*With every breath,*
*You go deeper into a hypnotic trance,*
*Deeper and deeper with every breath.*

Blond-haired, I am a sailor called *Simon.*
I've just been pushed off a ship.
I can't swim. I'm drowning.
I've just gone under,
Swinging my limbs wildly around,
Sinking farther and farther
From the surface.

*Every breath*
*Takes you deeper into trance,*
*Deeper and deeper with every breath.*

There is a chest full of treasure—
Bits of jewelry, gold and silver;
Whatever riches you can think of

Scattered on the bottom.

And bones.

Many bones.

Others have died here.

They don't want you to tell

What you've seen, the bastards!


*Every breath*

*Takes you deeper still,*

*Deeper and deeper with every breath.*


Who knows how many lives

Have ceased as a half-garbled

Choke going overboard.

It's getting ever colder and colder.

I thrash helplessly;

My lungs are burning

With every gulp of water.


*You're sinking deeper and deeper now.*

*It's as though you can almost feel it happening.*


I can see a spinning funnel

Of fine white light;

There is much warmth and fuzziness.

How bizarre!

Never a stream of thought

About my family,

My mother and father,

Or my beloved siblings,

Or my forlorn hometown,

Or England and America,

Or the savage past, the fiery future

Which will never be known;,

Or my betrothed,

My friends and enemies.

Only that I won't get home

To confess what I know.

Home, sweet home …


*It's as though you can almost feel it happening.*

*Deeper and deeper with every breath.*


They'll never know my confession …

Or will they?

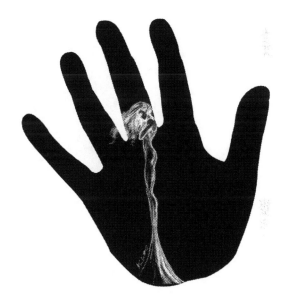

*Epilogue: Unraveling the Future*

PROTEUS: *Awake, oh, Lady of Green Stone,*

*Awake, for news awaits you.*

*For I have brought you*

*Flesh and bone,*

*Your progeny, your children.*

APHRODITE: *I curse the day*

*The Lord gave sight*

*To you, the hidden ferret,*

*Who razes with your scythe*

*All night*

*And quashes my trust,*

*My merit.*

*You made a solemn oath to me,*

*Why won't you*

*Keep your promise?*

*You called our Father*

*As your judge,*

*Twelve stars you called*

*To witness.*

*That should your silent*

*Dagger speak*

*Against my best, my oldest,*

*You'd bring the bravest*

*Son I seek,*

*Where is my ninth, my boldest?*

PROTEUS: *Don't raise your voice,*

*Oh Aphrodite,*

*Oh, foam born of Uranus,*

*For in this jelloid sea of mine*

*Your Simon sleeps in silence.*

*His eyes are lead,*

*His will runs weak;*

*In Hades an intruder.*

*That cunning egregore you seek,*

*Your Matthew and my Judah.*

APOSTOLOS:     *My mother, it is I, your son,*

*Your bravest of good measures,*

*The one you sent so far away*

*To bring back sunken treasures.*

APHRODITE:     *My son where have your*

*Good looks gone?*

*Your dark brown hair all faded?*

APOSTOLOS:     *I fear I lost those years ago*

*All pallid now and jaded.*

APHRODITE:     *I smell the plot of Proteus,*

*You reek of must, of rile.*

*Your bloodshot eyes*

*Your crumpled skin,*

*My beauty they defile.*

APOSTOLOS:     *Have you not heard*

*A dead man sing?*

*Not heard of living mortar?*

|  |  |
|---|---|
|  | *For all I yearned for was a spring* |
|  | *To put my lips to water.* |
| PROTEUS: | *Forbidden knowledge* |
|  | *You disclosed* |
|  | *In fifty-two reactions.* |
|  | *Confess it all as vengeful lies* |
|  | *And I'll undo my actions.* |
|  | *I took an oath not long ago,* |
|  | *To thrive in sin and pleasure* |
|  | *And split the silver cords of those* |
|  | *Who surmount wealth* |
|  | *And treasure.* |
| APOSTOLOS: | *Don't ask me how* |
|  | *I know, oh fiend,* |
|  | *Such things we must not question!* |
|  | *That felt-tip pen of yours I used* |
|  | *To hasten your detention.* |
| APHRODITE: | *Your talents are innumerable;* |
|  | *Your will a bar of iron,* |
|  | *But heed my words, oh Proteus,* |
|  | *Oh, morbid son of Prion.* |
|  | *I bore nine eagle sons of flight* |
|  | *I have no others for you.* |
|  | *That front of yours* |
|  | *The gallant knight,* |
|  | *I know your ill intentions.* |

*Do well to leave my sons alone*

*Or you'll behold my fury.*

*It matters not which ones you take*

*In time they'll be your jury.*

*And in the end, vain Proteus,*

*Behind the veil and curtain.*

*My Ennead will walk again,*

*Of that you can be certain.*

*I'll raise my children*

*From the ground,*

*When roses come to season.*

*I'll call on powers dignified*

*To fill their hearts with reason.*

*As nine wise men*

*They'll rule the world,*

*They'll open mind to travel.*

*From deep inside*

*The caves of earth*

*Their third eye I'll unravel.*

*Heed my words, old nemesis,*

*Oh foremost of Belial;*

*The mighty Will and Word of God*

*Cannot be put on trial.*

*And when the Golden Age*

*does dawn*

*I'll scry the old world's stillness,*

*To prove to you that*

*The seed and sword*

*Cannot be crushed by illness.*

*My Lord, give me reason to carry on*

*When I find myself dishonored*

*And stripped of all dignity;*

*Standing at the last frontier*

*Before a swift surrender*

*To an abyss of no return,*

*To bottomless fears that life*

*Will refuse me my right*

*To dream and hope,*

*As a being of the light*

*To aspire and just be.*


*My Lord, what is there left to do?*

*At most I beseech your flame.*

*Continue to burn within,*

*For I fear tomorrow*

*I shall awake*

*Without You*

*And all grace will be lost.*

To unveil truth and purpose
In this three-dimensional reality,
One must venture deep into
The uncharted territories of the primordial ocean
Where the ancient enemy lies asleep ...

*The ancient enemy sleeps ...*